D0577413

Mommies Say Shhh!

PATRICIA POLACCO

Mommies Say Shhh!

PARK COUNTY PUBLIC LIBRARY
Lake George Branch
37900 Hwy. 24
Lake George, CO 80827

Philomel Books
New York

Birds say cheep, cheep, cheep.

Squirrels say chee, chee, chee.

Bunnies say nothing at all.

Dogs say buff, buff, buff.

Sheep say baa, baa, baa.

Geese say honk, honk, honk.
Bunnies say nothing at all.

PARK COUNTY
PUBLIC LIBRARY

Chickens say cluck, cluck, cluck.

Ducks say quack, quack, quack.

Goats say ma-a-a, ma-a-a, ma-a-a.
Bunnies say nothing at all.

Cows say moo, moo, moo.

Cats say meow, meow, meow.

Pigs say oink, oink, oink.

Horses say neigh, neigh, neigh.

Everyone says cluck cluck, honk honk, quack quack, moo moo, ma-a-a ma-a-a, buff buff, meow meow, baa baa, oink oink, neigh neigh, chee chee, cheep cheep. . . .

Mommies say shhh, shhh, shhh.
And bunnies say nothing at all.

PAR COUNTY
PUBLIC LIBRARY

Patricia Lee Gauch, editor

Copyright © 2005 by Babushka Inc.
All rights reserved. This book, or parts thereof, may not be reproduced in any form without permission
in writing from the publisher, PHILOMEL BOOKS, a division of Penguin Young Readers Group,
345 Hudson Street, New York, NY 10014.
Philomel Books, Reg. U.S. Pat. & Tm. Off. The scanning, uploading and distribution of this book via the Internet
or via any other means without the permission of the
publisher is illegal and punishable by law. Please purchase only authorized electronic editions, and do not
participate in or encourage electronic piracy of copyrighted materials. Your support of the author's rights is appreciated.
Published simultaneously in Canada. Manufactured in China by South China Printing Co. Ltd.
Designed by Semadar Megged. Text set in 20-point Goudy. The illustrations are rendered in pencil and watercolor.
Library of Congress Cataloging-in-Publication Data
Polacco, Patricia. Mommies say shhh / Patricia Polacco. p. cm.
Summary: Animals make many different noises, but when they make too much noise, their mommies quiet them down.
[1. Animal sounds—Fiction. 2. Domestic animals—Fiction. 3. Mother and child—Fiction.] I. Title.
PZ7.P75186Mo 2005 [E]—dc22 2004009459
ISBN 0-399-24341-0
1 3 5 7 9 10 8 6 4 2
First Impression